The  Book

by Lynn Maslen Kertell
pictures by Sue Hendra and John R. Maslen

Scholastic Inc.
New York • Toronto • London • Auckland • Sydney • Mexico City • New Delhi • Hong Kong • Buenos Aires

Cat

COW

"Would you care for carrot cake?"

says cow to cat.

Dog

ducks

A delighted dog dashes

after dripping ducks.

The carrot cake distracts the dog.

Delicious!

Look for these **c** and **d** words in this book.

cake	dashes
care	delicious
carrot	delighted
cat	distracts
cow	dog
	dripping
	ducks

Look for these additional **c** and **d** words in the pictures: car, cherries, cherry tree, chimneys, clouds, cups, daffodils, and daisies.